W9-BCG-094

THE BAG
I'M TAKING
TO GRANDMA'S

by **Shirley Neitzel**

pictures by
Nancy Winslow Parker

Greenwillow Books, New York

For Scott and Jeffrey
—S. N.
**For Fats, who likes
to pack bags, too**
—N. W. P.

Black pen, watercolor paints,
and colored pencils were used
for the full-color art.
The text type is Seagull.

Grateful acknowledgment is made
to Tyco Toys, Inc., and its subsidiary
Matchbox International Limited ("Dinky
Sunbeam Alpine"); and to Buddy L Inc.,
for permission to illustrate their toy cars
in this book.

Library of Congress
Cataloging-in-Publication Data
Neitzel, Shirley.
    The bag I'm taking to Grandma's /
by Shirley Neitzel;
pictures by Nancy Winslow Parker.
        p.   cm.
Summary: In cumulative verses and
rebuses a young boy and his mother
have different views on how to pack
a bag for a trip to Grandma's.
ISBN 0-688-12960-9 (trade).
ISBN 0-688-12961-7 (lib. bdg.)
[1. Travel—Fiction.
2. Luggage—Fiction.
3. Rebuses. 4. Stories in rhyme.]
I. Parker, Nancy Winslow, ill. II. Title.
PZ8.3.N34Bag   1995   [E]—dc20
94-4115   CIP   AC

Here is the bag I'm taking to Grandma's.

Here is my mitt for playing ball

that I'll pack in the I'm taking

to Grandma's.

Here are my cars (I'm taking them all),

along with my for playing ball,

that I'll pack in the I'm taking

to Grandma's.

Here is my shuttle with the astronaut crew

that I'll stash with my 🚗 (I'm taking them all),

along with my 🧤 for playing ball,

that I'll pack in the 🛍 I'm taking

to Grandma's.

Here are the animals, two by two,

that ride in the with the astronaut crew

that I'll stash with my (I'm taking them all),

along with my for playing ball,

that I'll pack in the I'm taking

to Grandma's.

Here is the bunny I sleep with at night,

who guards the   two by two,

that ride in the with the astronaut crew

that I'll stash with my (I'm taking them all),

along with my for playing ball,

that I'll pack in the I'm taking

to Grandma's.

Here is my pillow, fluffy and light,

where I cuddle the I sleep with at night,

who guards the two by two,

that ride in the with the astronaut crew

that I'll stash with my (I'm taking them all),

along with my for playing ball,

that I'll pack in the I'm taking

to Grandma's.

Here is the book I want to read,

propped on my fluffy and light,

where I cuddle the I sleep with at night,

who guards the two by two,

that ride in the with the astronaut crew

that I'll stash with my (I'm taking them all),

along with my for playing ball,

that I'll pack in the I'm taking

to Grandma's.

Here is the flashlight I really need

to shine on the I want to read,

propped on my fluffy and light,

where I cuddle the I sleep with at night,

who guards the two by two,

that ride in the with the astronaut crew

that I'll stash with my (I'm taking them all),

along with my for playing ball,

that I'll pack in the I'm taking

to Grandma's.

Here is my mother who said, "Ready, hon?

"What's in this bag? It weighs a ton.

"Is this flashlight something you really need?

"Grandma has plenty of books to read.

"You're taking your bunny? Well, all right.

"But leave the pillow for just one night.

"You've got enough animals to stock a zoo!

"Leave them home, and your space shuttle, too.

"Choose one car. You can't take them all.

"And leave your mitt. There's no playing ball
in the apartment house at Grandma's.

"Now put in your slippers
and pack these clothes."

"But, Mother,

"I don't have room for those

in the bag I'm taking to Grandma's."